The Fifth Commandment

The Fifth Commandment

Eve Gaal

Copyright (C) 2016 Eve Gaal
Layout design and Copyright (C) 2016 Creativia (www.creativia.org)
Published 2016 by Creativia
Cover art by Creative Paramita
This book is a work of fiction. Names, characters, places, and incidents are the product of the author's imagination or are used fictitiously. Any resemblance to actual events, locales, or persons, living or dead, is purely coincidental.
All rights reserved. No part of this book may be reproduced or transmitted in any form or by any means, electronic or mechanical, including photocopying, recording, or by any information storage and retrieval system, without the author's permission.
evegaal@gmail.com

"Honor thy father and thy mother...."

Acknowledgements

My fiction work, The Fifth Commandment, can be considered either religious or paranormal fantasy. Let me just say, I'm not more religious or spiritual than any average person, but this is a story about being a kid. I have to admit I was a mischievous, somewhat rebellious child. (At least that's what they said.) Now that I'm a 'mature woman', I realize I'm not guiltier or holier than anyone else is– or was –in fact—I consider myself a humble, if flawed individual, hoping for forgiveness and looking forward to the promised afterlife. My graduate degree is in Human Behavior, not theology. I want to thank all my amazing teachers and would love to mention a long list of 'men of the cloth' who inspired me in many ways but feel they may not support my divine story, as most of it came to me in my dreams.

I often wonder whether God gets bored of our lackluster and monotonous excuses about being human. After all, it's our human-ness that separates us from being angels or gods. He may also think it's cute the same way animal behavior separates dogs, cats and all animals from humans. We enjoy watching them dance and sing online and by being imperfect, they create wonderful and often humorous entertainment.

Peter denied Jesus three times and yet, Jesus forgave him for everything. He forgives all of us for everything we do and that forgiveness inspired this novella. I hope you like it or at least find it entertaining and if you enjoyed it then I'm thanking you in advance for your short review.

Maybe something will make you relate to the guilt associated with being a teenager and wishing for different parents. Not that you, or anyone you'd know would ever think of something like that! (Smiling) Of course, I'd like to thank my angel parents and hope they forgive me for pushing my boundaries.

I'd like to thank my publisher and my talented online writing friends and blog followers for all your supportive, encouraging comments. Thank you to my best friend Yvonne for selecting the imperfect me to be Godmother to your twins. Additionally, I have to add a big thank you to my beta reader from Chicago, Dr. Amy Fremgen and my loving husband, Steve who showers me with love every day.

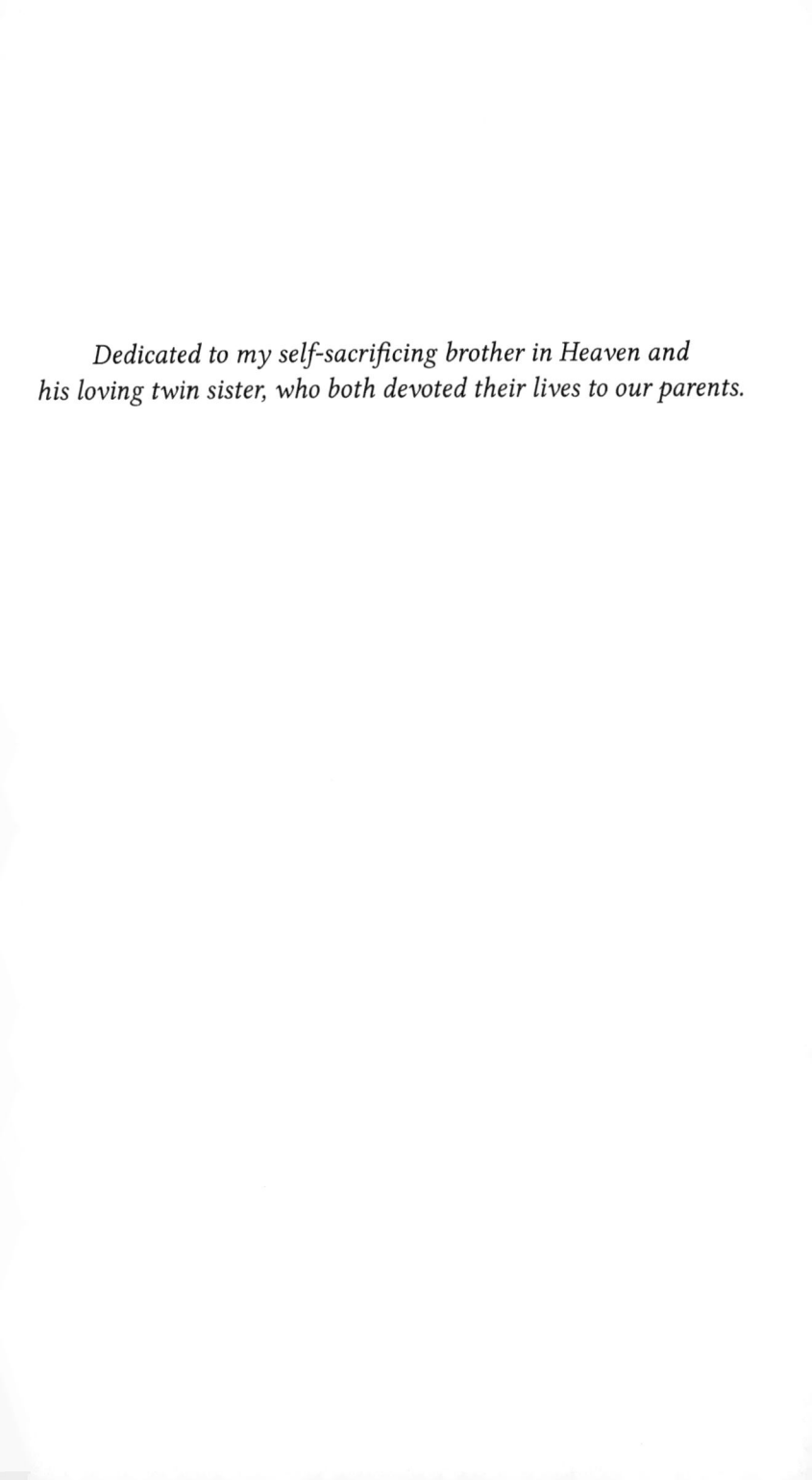

*Dedicated to my self-sacrificing brother in Heaven and
his loving twin sister, who both devoted their lives to our parents.*

Prologue

A taxi speeds through Rome, Italy and a soprano's voice wafts from the tinny sounding radio, singing Puccini's famous aria, 'O Mio Babbino Caro'. It's a muggy summer day and groups from all over the world are crowding into Vatican Square. The music surges but the fast driving cab swerves, accidentally crashing into a group of tourists. Though the lyrics,'mi struggo emi tormento! O Dio, vorrei morir—Babbo, pieta, pieta!' continues to fill the piazza, it is obvious that something serious and most likely fatal has happened. Toddlers scatter, mothers chase after them and groups of nuns hurry like groups of penguins towards the entrance of St. Peter's Basilica. Blood drips slowly into the cobblestone crevices, pooling savagely around a designer purse. Women and children are screaming and crying. Heated male voices are yelling in Italian for the crowd to move away from the scene. The sound of an approaching European ambulance blends its annoying wail almost in tempo with the music. Minutes later, we hear the scratchy sound of a television announcer talking about the crash that took the life of a girl from Beverly Hills, California. The police have pulled the driver from the cab and while cuffing him, the dissonance changes to colorful and upbeat music that sounds vaguely like Panamanian calypso.

Chapter One

Christina didn't like the sensation of freefalling from the sky. No visible threads were holding her above her parent's suburban home in Normal, Illinois. The feeling reminded her of a roller coaster ride going haywire, except she had feathers lodged between her front teeth making her think maybe she had eaten the contents of her pillow and entered a disturbing nightmare. Unfortunately, it wasn't a dream at all but some kind of spiritual journey. Guilt, made her think she deserved all of it and more. This wild shot through the sky had turned her into a freefalling piece of space junk or the embodiment of a twisted piece of penance as punishment for her transgressions and mild but slightly evil, teenage thoughts. Whatever it was, her current situation had her corporeal body whirling through the atmosphere at a horrific and unpleasant speed. Needless to say, no one heard her screams.

As she fell, she tried making sense of the immense ordeal that had taken control of her life in the most unusual ways. Her everyday reality had become some kind of paranormal or existential situation that had evolved into recent encounters with strange people, new places, religious icons, angels– possibly demons–intent on literally turning her world upside down. There were no fantasy castles, wizards, goblins or magical spells to make her think she read it in a book. There were no unicorns, rainbows and tiny trolls from fairytales that might have lodged into the crevices of her imagination. Nonetheless, screaming felt so much better than trying to figure things out. "Help...I'm sorry...for...everything...." As she gasped out the words, she began to remember how everything stemmed from that one day. The day she wore her ripped jeans and had a fight with her mom about how to dress for school. *Thank goodness for friends,* she had thought, punching in Molly's number.

"Oh my God, my parents are so weird. I just can't take it anymore," she had said to Mollie who lived like a spoiled princess in Bloomington with her poodles and ballet classes.

"Yeah, I know how you feel," she replied, trying to sound like she could relate. "Where's your Mom from anyway? She has a cute accent."

"Cute? Blech. There's nothing even vaguely cute about either one of them. I wish I had different parents. Normal ones like yours...." That was it. The moment she uttered those words her life had changed. All of her friends had told her they had wanted different parents, it was a typical conversation starter and something to text message or blog about. Meanwhile, her throat felt hoarse screaming and praying to different saints, while feathers lodged in her throat. Was this supposed to teach her a lesson? Had she learned anything? "I'll be good...I promise...." The wind tore the words from her mouth as she clung to her purse above Redbird Arena and Epiphany Catholic Church. "Oh my God...can anyone hear me?" Panic filled her as she looked out over the foggy horizon dotted with tiny clouds. "Please...help...if anyone up there can hear me?" she yelled to no one in particular, as the Amtrak to Chicago drowned out her voice.

The irony of living in a town called Normal seemed to be obvious to everyone but Christina's ethnic parents. Everyone, even her whack-job of a drama coach knew that nothing was "normal" in Normal. The town was like a giant crossword puzzle with tricky question marks tossed in to keep everyone guessing the truth. *How normal is Normal?* No one knew all the hidden abnormalities, but the obvious things stood out like an infected and blistering boil. Most 'normal' towns with shops and taller buildings for example, called the central area, 'downtown' rather than 'Uptown' as in Normal. Weirder still, was that America's only Mitsubishi manufacturing plant was turning out SUV's with the help of Mollie's rich mom. As if Mollie's mom couldn't just stay at home, playing with those spoiled, curly haired dogs, she had to go to work and flaunt her fashionable wardrobe all over town. And why would an Asian car company put a gigantic auto factory in a place where women outnumbered men? Do women like building cars better than men? Is it all part of some mysterious irony? Is that why they go to nursing school at the University of Illinois? And why do women in her town of Normal outnumber men anyway? On top of everything else, her family had to be Catholic, which made things even more bizarre.

Why did her Mom think wearing thong underwear was a sin? Or the fact that she wanted fashionably cool, torn jeans that covered all the important parts of her anatomy. Allegedly, these strategic holes invited boys to think bad thoughts. Didn't boys think bad thoughts anyway? Her hems were inches longer than Molly's dresses and her jeans were looser. She never brought up anything regarding a school play or cheer tryouts because she already knew the answer. Where did her parents get this stuff? *They should have locked her in a basement and thrown away the keys.*

Even more bewildering was the local paper called *The Pantagraph*. Wasn't it hard enough selling newspapers during the internet age just being *the Times* or the *Post?* Was *Pantagraph* Latin, or was everything in the world turning Greek? Being a kid in the United States meant learning and respecting other cultures while maintaining your own identity. Bad enough she heard her mother praying and singing in her wildly complicated native tongue and if she tried learning one of those tongue twisting words, her mother scolded her, telling her to speak English! With Christina's recent religious encounter looming above, the next thing she expected were lessons in Aramaic.

An endless maelstrom of questions swirled around in her mind, reminding her of how abnormal the past few minutes had been. Were they minutes exactly or had time become skewed like some science fiction movie trying to portray a parallel universe, where nothing was normal? She hated those movies because she didn't see the point. Why would anyone waste two good hours in an ice-cold theater with a sticky floor and greasy red-velvet curtains drooping from absorbed popcorn oil, to watch a duplicate portrayal of Earth's various problems? During her descent to Earth, she knew in her heart that this was not science fiction. In fact, it was some shape-shifting form of her personal reality, but who would believe any of this?

Her naturalized parents and their constant stories of coming to America from the "old country" didn't answer any of her questions. Sure, they had hardships and giant obstacles to overcome, but did they ever have to endure a mouth full of feathers while cascading through a cloud? She didn't doubt their perseverance, their fortitude, even their love, but she needed answers and she needed them now. Now, before she sideswiped the blooming dogwoods growing outside her church.

Miraculously, the wind gusts swept her lean legs and slim body gently over the trees and steeple, bouncing her through large double doors where she landed standing, upright in front of a small door without a scratch or bruise. Opening the door to the confessional, she inhaled before plopping down to take a deeper breath on a worn, wooden bench. Children didn't know exhaustion, but this time, for the first time in her life, Christina felt tired way beyond her years.

Chapter Two

"I heard you my child, please continue." Father Joe's reassuring voice echoed through the tiny window of the confessional. Christina rubbed her eyes adjusting to the dimly lit wooden sanctuary.

Caught off guard she didn't know what to say. "Whoa, how did I? Oh dear…" Christina coughed, trying to clear her throat while stalling for time. "Never mind…ah… what did you say?" She glanced around uncertain as to how she landed so magically into such comfortable and familiar surroundings. One minute ago, her body could have splattered across College Avenue and yet here she was speaking to one of her favorite priests, all in one whole but windblown piece. She automatically crossed herself and looked up at the ceiling as the blood returned back into her feet from her head. Her messed up, confused head that had tendrils of fine hair sticking out all over the place. As she smoothed down her tangled hair, Father Joe asked the expected question as she mumbled her act of contrition.

"Are you aware of any sins you've committed my little one?" He sounded so calm and happy, as if he really loved his job and especially the afterlife benefits. It took him a few minutes to place the voice of the out of breath young lady sitting in the adjacent booth but after years of listening to confessions, he had a knack for reading voices and felt confident he knew exactly who sat on the other side.

"Not anything different than last month. I bought a new tube of gloss at the drugstore and Mom said I looked in the mirror too long, so I guess that's the sin of vanity. I'm sorry." She paused and thought about other sins but so much had happened since the last time she came to church she almost forgot everything. "I ate too much at Sunday dinner. Please forgive my gluttony," she whispered. "And Molly–I think I'm jealous–she's my BFF—I mean best friend. I can't believe her mom is letting her go to the Coachella Music festival in California."

She heard him clear his throat with a sound of agreement. Molly didn't attend his church but he knew Christina's friend lived in a Tudor style mansion in a country club, on the outskirts of Bloomington. The sprawling home on forest-filled acreage had a brick circular driveway and overlooked lakes and sand traps. Being envious sounded reasonable and rather human.

"Father, I think the main reason I'm here is because of my reoccurring problems where I dream of an easier life at home. I feel my parents are too strict. In fact, I'm convinced that they are entirely too old-fashioned. Is that a sin, Father?" Her voice quivered and she felt her toes curl up inside of her shoes.

"How do you mean, please explain?" Father Joe sounded so kind and loving. She had always felt like she could tell him anything. But this—this—might be more than she should admit to anyone.

"Well, you know my parents and… And how different they are," Christina began.

"Yes, I know your parents my dear…" he paused, before admitting he recognized her voice. "They came to live here exactly when you were born. This is Christina right?"

"Yes, it's me Father," she squeaked out her answer with a hoarse, throaty voice that felt parched from the earlier blast of air and feathers. She couldn't remember where she had her last meal and her last sip of water. Foggy and unnerving visions were making her anxious. She thought about leaving, running from the church, but the reassuring voice of the priest kept her holding onto the built-in pew.

Father Joe sounded throaty too but in a different way. His raspy voice had an aging Irish resonance. "In fact, I baptized you as an infant, a wee one like I've rarely ever seen. He smiled at the memory of all the babies in his mind. Baptisms were his favorite. "Anyway, how do you mean, different? Are you trying to say that they won't let you do all the things other kids your age do? If you like music, we have a wonderful youth program for teens on Thursday nights; maybe you'd like to join something like that?" Christina was quiet as she listened to the helpful recommendations of the kind man behind the darkened panel. "Would your parents allow you to come together with other young folk and sing in the choir perhaps? Doug Barnes from your school plays quite a nice electric version of **How Great Thou Art** and the **Glory Be** on his guitar. You know Doug, don't you? I'm sure they'd love to have more singers Christina."

He would have continued with more ideas but she finally interrupted with, "Yes, I know Doug." She thought of the cool looking kid who always wore sunglasses and remembered his dad being a rock star from Lincoln Park. "But no, Father Joe, I don't think that's the problem. They *are* strict but the truth is I'm just embarrassed by their accents and their University teaching jobs at Illinois State!" There, she said it and admitted her painful burden. She crossed herself and waited for lightning and thunder to strike her to the ground. She knew disrespecting her parents had caused everything. It had brought her to the confessional. It had turned her life upside down. If not lightning and thunder, then another gust of wind might come to take her away with more clouds and more feathers.

Father Joe sounded like he was smiling again, "Is that all or is there more?"

"Oh dear…" Christina felt like she could go on forever… "Yes there's more, a lot more." She might as well admit to the curse or whatever it happened to be and go all the way. She had caused all of it– and after everything that had happened–she was willing to take responsibility for her actions. Even thinking it was a curse could get her into trouble—it was actually more of a lifetime lesson or a supernatural spell. A jinx? She had to measure her words and be careful, because she wanted to stay grounded, even if it meant facing humiliation and shame caused by the error of her ways.

"They eat spicy, unusual things; they don't understand my homework even though they're teachers… Oh, Father Joe…they are on a completely different planet. They understand the metaphysical universe, but have trouble with this basic, regular world we live in." She inhaled before storming on into the uncharted waters of deep, ungodly sin. Perhaps she had died anyway and it didn't matter. Father Joe deserved to know because he controlled the souls of his parishioners, her parents and what was left of her own. Even if, she supposed, her own soul was thoroughly wicked and possibly damned to eternal flames in the netherworld.

"Go on," the priest was listening intently but he glanced at his watch. So far, she wasn't even up to one Hail Mary and two Our Fathers. He made a mental note of her use of the word metaphysical and thought he might give her a compliment later on for using good vocabulary words.

"My friends make fun of me. My Mom's glasses look like they're from the '50's and my Dad even wears a pocket protector for goodness sake!" No one understood the pain she suffered. Belting out the embarrassment felt like unloading a rowboat filled with cement blocks. "Have you seen her glasses? They look like something out of a scary movie!" Every word made her feel better. "My parents are geeks!"

Even though his mind wandered, Father Joe kept on listening intently. He knew these young people didn't have too many places to vent. Still, he had things to do: a bulletin to write, a fish fry to plan and another homily. "Christina, I know kids can be tough, but so far you haven't said anything that sounds like a mortal or venial sin. You **do** honor them as your parents, right? Don't forget the fifth Commandment little one."

Christina cringed at the words 'fifth commandment' but kept on going, "Well I hate sauerkraut and sausages and I'm tired of being called a Pole-lock." It had come out a bit louder than she expected, but what was she supposed to do? She had to deal with so many stupid things at home it had impassioned her confession to a feverish pitch that may have discomfited Father Joe. Worst of all, she almost cussed in the confessional. Meanwhile, people like *Mollie and Doug Barnes* had no such trouble and ate normal food with normal parents, both of whom had normal jobs.

"OK, OK, I think I'm starting to understand," Father Joe wasn't smiling now, he was very serious. "I have an accent Christina; I'm from Ireland as you know. Sometimes I like Irish stew, even a spot of Irish whiskey now and then. Does that make me weird, Christina?"

By repeating her name twice, she knew he was serious. "No, Father Joe that's different," she shifted a bit in the warm confines of the confessional, realizing she would have to come clean. Irish people had parades and drank green beer on St. Pat's. Irish people were acceptable immigrants. He had no idea what she went through.

"Well now, how in the world is that different Christina, answer me that?" He sounded a bit annoyed, perhaps bordering on anger. He didn't have time for her childlike shenanigans. She thought about what she was going to say and swallowed. Her mouth felt parched and dry like a western landscape in need of rain, due to her previous ranting above Mclean County. She forced out the truth but almost gagged on the last word, her mouth agape like a fish out of water. *Could he handle the truth? He was an adult–an educated man–a priest and a pastor. For God's sake, he had to handle it!*

In a serious tone, she summed up her declaration: "I didn't honor them, Father. I made the mistake several times," she paused out of fear or perhaps for affect, "of wishing for different…parents." Her head began to hurt and she felt horrible. Goosebumps ran up and down her arm and her stomach danced like a moth hitting a lamppost. Maybe telling Father Joe wasn't such a good idea. All of a sudden, it seemed quiet. She could hear pigeons in the courtyard and a thumping in her chest that felt like it was ready to explode. Her feet wanted to flee all the way to Lake Michigan but something kept her rooted, her fingers now clasped in prayer. She needed to hear her penance and anticipated the worst.

Father Joe inched closer to the partition in the confessional and asked, "Did you just say you made the mistake of wishing for different parents? My hearing is not what it used to be. At first I thought you wished for some parrots."

If he was making a joke, she didn't find it funny. "No, you're right, Father Joe, I'm ashamed to admit it, but I wished for new parents and a lot of very strange things have happened to me since. I'd like to explain if you have the time." Her voice shook and she sounded like she was going to begin sobbing any minute. Crying in a confessional sounded so ridiculously childish that Christina wanted to get a hold of her sanity while awaiting Father Joe's comments and hopefully he'd believe her. He had to help her. Her mind reeled from the unusual circumstances surrounding her admission and the fact that he heard parrots instead of parents made her even more upset. "Oh Father Joe…"

Fortunately, Father Joe liked the big-boned girl who hadn't made eye contact with him since confirmation. Outside of the fact that she wore too much makeup and too much black clothing, she was a bright girl in school with a lot of potential. Her parents were tall, proud Europeans who defected to the United States to seek freedom and happiness from a communist ruled government that persecuted the faithful and most people considered intellectuals. They had wanted nothing but the best life for their tiny, premature born daughter, Christina. A wonderful, healthy life filled with all the wonders of the American dream. Perhaps one day, they hoped, she would meet a nice German-American or Polish-American boy and they would be blessed with adorable grandchildren. In all actuality, they were the nicest parents anyone could ever have and he looked forward to the day he could stand in front of her family and watch her walk down the aisle. Not only did he look forward to seeing her get married but he also looked forward to the day he would baptize her baby. Father Joe loved baptisms.

Months before her baptism, he had seen the mother, Irena, praying the Rosary on her swollen knees in front of the Virgin's statue. It had been a cold January day prior to Christina's birth. He was on call that evening and recalled driving through a storm to the hospital. That long winter night the doctor quickly explained he may have to administer last rites to a stillborn. Fortunately, that didn't happen and Christina grew into a lovely girl with a distant, slightly guarded family who came late to Mass and slipped out the side doors afterwards, avoiding the usual greetings and free donuts.

"Let's go to my office Christina where you can give me the rest of your entire explanation. OK?" Father Joe exited the confessional and opened her side letting her into the church where stained glass windows sparkled in the afternoon sun, multiplying into rainbows of color in splendid beams above the pews. The prism of colors bounced off the crucifix holding Jesus in a path of light that looked divine. It had to be true. The things that had happened had happened for a reason. Christina knew she had to tell her story and whether or not Father Joe believed her, was strictly in God's hands. She patted down her flyaway hair and blinked several times, her eyes adjusting to the light. The story he would hear would not be anywhere near what he would, or could have anticipated. In actuality, it might create doubt in his heart and shake the firmament he stood upon, but he didn't know that yet. At this point, he simply felt that perhaps listening to a young parishioner could help reaffirm the job security he so desperately needed.

Father Joe was short and balding, with a dry sense of humor. His occasional mood swings made him work extra hard, because he knew no one tolerated cranky or unusual behavior in the priesthood, especially after the recent and costly maelstrom of scandals surrounding the church. The allegations were so severe that they had rocked the very foundation of Christianity which had taken ages to build. A foundation started by Peter, the apostle of Jesus.

Father Joe's personal troubles seemed to stem from somewhat manageable vices such as a horrible diet, infused with daily doses of alcohol. He looked upon being human as his crutch—one he wore proudly on his shoulders—a sort of victim of circumstances. Still, he took his job very seriously because he had been transferred one too many times. This was his last chance according to the Bishop. If this stint as Pastor of Epiphany didn't work out he had to retire or move to the Philippines where they had a huge shortage of priests. Going to the Philippines, where he imagined it hot and humid all the time, didn't sound like any option to look forward to. Besides, heat and humidity brought out bugs, and Father Joe who loved everyone and everything; hated only one thing and that was bugs! All of them–even butterflies and ladybugs—but especially spiders—he hated them most of all.

He consoled himself with the thought that by playing his cards right; everything at St Epiphs would work out just fine.

Heck, he also thought about how much better life was in the suburbs, where he could fly low to the ground, out from under the radar of the Chicago inquisition. Politics and old-fashioned thinking ran the cathedrals over there. He wasn't up to playing the games of protocol and the cardinal-red, taped-up bureaucracy. Little did Father Joe know that this game had special cards from a new, slicker deck–they were also intangible and being dealt by God.

They walked through the flowery courtyard, disrupting the gawking, judgmental pigeons that seemed to stare at Christina as if they knew about her guilt. Inside the office, Father Joe raised the blinds to let in some light and guided her to a large burgundy leather chair across from his desk. She looked around at the books, the clock ticking on the wall and teetering piles of extra church bulletins balancing on a corner shelf. Next, she saw Father Joe pour whiskey into an etched, Waterford glass. After making himself comfortable, he sat back and said, "OK, my child, please tell me what happened?"

Chapter Three

Thank God, Father Joe is having a drink, Christina thought. It would act like a teaspoon of sugar and coat all her far-fetched and melodramatic sounding memories which, though true, needed a dose of something strong to sound realistic. After hearing her account, she imagined he'd probably want to try something stronger, like smoking crack or snorting coke. Maybe she would be single-handedly responsible for turning the church into a crack house. It starts with little things and pretty soon, no one shows for mass—except maybe her mom. They close the church down and it doesn't sell to anyone. They try to list it online but no one wants an old church in a bad neighborhood. It happened in Boston, L.A. and Detroit. No more Polish Mass, Italian Mass, or German Mass. The Sun had an article about how old bilingual churches were fading away. Her mom would just have to drive to the nice cathedral in Chicago and meet dad for dinner. It's a win-win. Once the pimps and hookers find out it's empty, the rest is history. She smiled inwardly at the image in her head of Father Joe being handcuffed and hauled from the rectory. *"It's her fault," he'd say pointing towards Christina. "She made me lose my mind!"*

Christina had never experimented with drugs, not even marijuana like Doug and Mollie but she knew what they were, and she knew being under the influence altered thinking in the worse imaginable way. The thought of Father Joe in a drug-induced stupor almost made her laugh. Obviously, after floating through space above Normal this morning, she didn't need any drugs to get high.

She put her hands on her cheeks, forcing herself to look serious. "Anyway, Father Joe, I wanted to explain about St. Peter's Basilica in Rome."

"Excuse me Christina, but I don't really understand… what?" *Did she just mention the Vatican?* Father Joe sat down and grabbed a pencil and a piece of paper.

"I know it sounds strange since I never actually traveled outside of the United States but for some unexplainable reason I went there recently and saw all of it. I remember standing in front of a painting of St. Peter with a rooster. The painting must mean something personal or it's trying to tell me something, but I haven't figured out what it might be yet. As I tell my story, I hope to learn more about why certain things happened the way they did. Hopefully, you can help me.

Anyway, it was summer, I was older, and had nice shoes. I wore very expensive, adorable dresses. It was obvious I had a lot of money because of my cute styled hair, manicured nails and I even had a cell phone. You know–normal cool stuff for rich girls. I wasn't interested in the amazing tour involving the main altar, the Pieta, the veil of Veronica or Rafael's angels painted on the walls of the Sistine Chapel. Although there was the sweetest little coin purse with angels on it at the gift shop…" Christina stopped, realizing that the souvenir shop didn't add anything to the importance of her story. She waved a hand in the air and continued, "Never mind that. Sorry. I was tired and hungry and wanted nothing to do with all the gorgeous history and art. I was only interested in going to clubs or shops with friends. Father, this seems so odd now that I'm embarrassed explaining it to you."

Looking serious, Father Joe scribbled a few notes and asked, "Christina, was this a dream?" He wondered where she had gotten the travel information and said, "Are you studying Italy in school?" Then he thought about the internet and all the virtual tours and realistic games they offered. Somewhere far in the back corner of his mind was a growing, slightly gnawing fear about how he would report this counseling session to the Bishop's office. A tiny bead of sweat formed on his brow and he wiped it off with the back of his sleeve.

Her gaze bore into the watery pools of Father Joe's eyes. "No, Father, we are not studying Italy and this wasn't a dream! This really happened to me. Remember I said, I was older and all I wanted to do was meet up with friends who were going to take me to some dance clubs in Rome?"

"Christina, I believe you, but I am painstakingly confused." He raised his right hand into the air for affect but quickly returned his clasp around the glass. "We both know you're too young for dance clubs. Where were your parents? What happened next?" The glass beckoned, though almost empty and Christina felt like getting up to refill it because her incredulous story was just about to become even more dubious. What if he thought she was a crazy witch or agnostic heretic? Would he throw her out? Could she be excommunicated?

She quietly mumbled a silent prayer and burst out with an emotional appeal, "Father Joe, I want you to know I love Jesus and I believe in God with all my heart."

He didn't want to laugh because he knew she had always been a genuinely nice girl. Instead, he smiled. "Yes, my dear, I know that, I remember your confirmation too." He loudly sucked the last drop of whiskey out of the crystal glass. She stared at the prisms of color created by the sun's afternoon rays sparkling from facets surrounded by his short stubby fingers. The rainbows of color swirled like the ones that had bounced around in the sanctuary. Finally, her attention diverted from the crystal to the clock as it ticked softly, reminding Christina, she should continue.

"Well, I exited the Basilica near some tee-shirt and souvenir vendors when I realized I needed to find my hotel. There were so many people; tourists from all kinds of countries and groups of nuns. I'm out past Via di Porta Angelica, when I get run over by an Italian taxi. This maniac driver accidentally plows into a group of us." She looked at Father Joe's glass but didn't want to sound accusing so she averted her eyes and turned away. The high drama of it all made her put her head into her hands and she closed her eyes for a moment before saying, "He was probably drunk. Well anyway, that's how I died."

"Excuse me? You died?" Father Joe pulled his head up from his glass and his eyes looked watery and huge. After licking his lips to savor the last microscopic drop, he managed to say, "Christina, I'm speechless." He placed the empty leaded crystal carefully on the desk, "I'm not sure I understand this whole situation." Father Joe smiled inwardly thinking that seventeen year olds never grow up. "How did you know what the name of the road was and how did you finally appear here in front of me? That is, if you really died?"

She had to sound more convincing because she either never had it or she lost his attention somewhere. "That's when everything turned really weird Father. St. Peter himself stood above me with his arms folded, asking if I had learned anything from the previous incident. I had wings and sat on a soft cloud looking down through a mist above the Vatican." I saw the same crowds from high up in the air. I saw the taxi. I saw my own blood leaking onto the cobblestones.''

"Mmmm, go on." He listened intently and lifted a graying eyebrow, trying not to roll his eyes. "You said you had wings?"

"Yeah, it was really nice, I was light as a feather and I really enjoyed seeing all the things happening on Earth. I told St. Peter that I wasn't sure what I had learned, but all the signs indicated that maybe I had picked the wrong family."

"What?" Father Joe crossed himself. The phone on his desk began to ring. He picked it up and nervously answered the caller, "Yes, Father Andrew please bring Father George…we'll have lunch…yes…Oh–and by the way–I have a nice young lady in my office named Christina– I'd love for all of you to meet." He laughed and said, "No nothing like that, but she does have some interesting things to share. Tomorrow then, at eleven, OK? OK. Goodbye."

Christina cringed at the thought of re-telling the beginning of her long story, but could tell by Father Joe's serious tone that Father Andrew and Father George would need to hear the whole thing. He set the phone slowly back into its cradle and looked at Christina with a loving but nonetheless pitiful stare. It must have been divine intervention, he thought, that caused Andrew to call at that precise moment, so he could graciously finish this torturous session with this misguided young lady.

"Oh Father Joe, you think I'm nuts, don't you? I can leave if you'd like so you don't have to hear any more of my sinful adventures. I think I told you it was a long story."

"Christina, please continue." Father Joe glanced at his watch and said, "I need to hear everything, especially since this was a religious experience you had. Tell me how you knew it was St. Peter? Did he look like the pictures you've seen of him? Did he have a beard?" Suppressing a grin, he tried to hold back any tone of sarcasm, but worried she may have detected a trace. Christina nodded at the last question, but Father Joe prodded. "Come on now, this is really a remarkable event, not too many people get to meet St. Peter and live a life on Earth to tell about it. Please continue now or we can continue tomorrow after school; either way, I want to hear the whole thing." He shook his head and didn't like seeing her pout. "You don't mind me asking a few of my friends to listen along with me do you?" He smiled, but being a perceptive child, she thought he looked like he was faking it. It didn't matter; she was tired, thirsty and hungry.

"No, I don't mind," she responded quickly. "I'll come back after school tomorrow and tell you and your friends the whole story. Just one more thing, St Peter told me that I must have really enjoyed California. Can you imagine Father Joe? I've never even been out of this state? He said I was speaking exactly like the locals. He also told me that each soul is gifted with one hundred years. Apparently, I had lived 25 years of my life in a selfish, spoiled person's body. I wanted to figure out why he had sent me to live with rich people in Beverly Hills. I asked St. Peter why he sent me there." Christina kept winding her long hair around her finger, nervous and excited that someone important was willing to listen to her drama. "But St. Peter, he told me," she inhaled deeply and sighed, 'I didn't send you to Beverly Hills. God did'."

"OK, Christina, now I'm even more confused. Don't forget I know you are only sixteen? Anyway, you have a long walk home, why don't you finish your story from this point tomorrow. I took notes and I'll bring my friends up to speed on everything you've told me so far." He moved his chair back and came around to Christina's side as she stood up. She wiped a tear from her eyes and felt defeated. She knew he didn't believe her but hoped for the best tomorrow. Wait until he hears the whole story, she thought with a sniffle. When he escorted her out of the office he asked about something stuck to her brown sweater. "Christina, what's this?" He picked it off and held it to the light. "It looks like a feather."

Chapter Four

When Christina arrived home, her parents were reading next to the fireplace in the living room. "We were worried about you young lady," her mother called out. "Go get your dinner, it's in the oven." The musical cadence of her mother's accent shot straight to her heart. A voice she longed for, needed and missed. A second later she added, "It might be cold by now. You should warm it up." Nothing had changed. If they only knew, what she had been through to come back to this street, this home and these parents—she felt like touching the worn wallpaper and kissing the shabby carpet.

She heard something she interpreted as a tinge of guilt, but didn't bite on it. Her dad was so absorbed in his technical data that he didn't look overly concerned about anything. She could set the house on fire before he would lift his eyes off his intricate proposals or technical manuals. "I'm not that hungry, mom, but I'll check it out." Truthfully, she was starving and her mouth watered as she walked to the oven and peered through the worn appliance's encrusted window. It looked like a casserole created from potatoes and onions with layers of bacon or sausage and grated cheese. It didn't matter. .. .She was hungry and happily devoured every lukewarm morsel. When finished, she scrubbed the earthenware dish and dried it before returning it to the bottom cupboard with the others. Later, as she tucked herself in and said her prayers, she gave thanks to God for giving her these parents and this life, rather than those other lives she had experienced in the last few cosmic days. Tomorrow, she would get it all off her chest and tell Father Joe everything.

Around four in the morning, she heard a voice resonating in her head. "Christina, it's St. Peter. Thank you for trying to explain everything to my church, but most of all congratulations on learning all the things you needed to learn. I promise the memory of all of this will go away, and only the love in your heart will remain. Goodnight dear child of God, have a wonderful day." Christina pulled back the covers and walked to the window. It was dark outside, but as she stared into the yard, she saw a tiny bird sitting on the ledge of the window looking into her room and tilting his adorable little eyes and beak to get a better look. Christina smiled, wandered back to bed, and fell into a deep sleep.

The next day, after school, she went to Father Joe's office as planned and sat across from him in his leather chair. Father Andrew and Father George were there as planned. They sat on smaller folding chairs near the door wanting to listen, but not wanting to distract Christina's thought processes. They smiled awkward smiles, introduced themselves and promised to listen to everything. She had never met the two visiting priests before, but immediately felt comfortable around them. Christina supposed if they were friends with her pastor, then they must be nice. They were both from Chicago and had taken the morning Amtrak train down to have lunch with Father Joe.

"So, Christina, you went somewhere in California? Please continue from where you left off."

She looked around the room and began to speak. "Father Joe, it is still quite a long story because St. Peter told me he had to send me back to Earth each time, until I learned my lesson. He told me—repeatedly—that each time we are blessed to receive one hundred years–sometimes a bit more. If we find our spiritual path, it might be shorter but I wasn't sure what that meant. For instance, he said, whether we figure everything out after a meager five days, five years or five decades, then we are back up there with him with a one-way ticket to Heaven."

St. Peter told me that it is only sad on Earth when a baby dies an infant death, but it is a surefire guarantee into God's Promised Land. I guess babies are smart when it comes to our feelings. Unfortunately, he also said that it usually takes closer to eighty years to learn our lessons." She mumbled, "I'm a bit confused about the years though…because I think I just spent eighty years somewhere myself." Somehow, they missed her last comment entirely, but she truly was mystified about time. She stared at the clock for reassurance, glad to be back in present day Normal, Illinois.

Eighty years? Christina seemed to want to know something about the concept of time but no one was prepared to answer her questions. They didn't really know what to say so they all looked over at Father Andrew because he had the grayest hair. "Yes, well, look at Father Andrew, he's getting up there," Father George joked. Everyone laughed except Christina.

They reminded her of the boys at school–no cares in the world and not very deep or understanding. In her mind's eye, she could almost envision all three of them at recess, pointing and laughing, before running to play dodge ball. If anything, her experiences had made her brave. After the things she had been through, she could face anything. But she knew she had to watch her attitude. Envisioning herself a purposeful gladiator, she could face and fight lions and even this pack of skeptics. Pursing her lips, she continued, "Since my entire future life was resting on this, I asked St. Peter what I needed to do to get to Heaven. I wondered if I picked the right parents or if I picked tougher conditions, would that make any difference?"

"Were you scared? Speaking to St. Peter sounds rather intimidating." Father Andrew noticed her serious tone and almost whispered his question.

"No, St. Peter smiled at me and told me I simply had to learn everything I could and be accepting of my conditions with an open heart full of unconditional love. Of course, I also had to follow all ten of God's commandments. Then he told me something interesting—maybe kind of strange. He said that even *he* couldn't go to Heaven because he was urgently needed at the Gate. I asked him if he could go there for a vacation and he admitted that he couldn't because of his denying Christ three times!" Her voice rose and her face felt flushed but she continued her impassioned speech, thinking she better get as much of this out as quickly as possible. "Though he was very humble and thankful for being honored on Earth as a teacher, gatekeeper and fisherman, it was the forgiveness he appreciated the most. Since Christ forgave him, Peter was so overjoyed that he was honored and happy to worry about every single soul and their individual journey into life everlasting. To Peter, I think it's like fishing. Every person that enters the Kingdom of God is another catch." Now she smiled tenderly at these men of the cloth and hoped she could hold their attention by getting personal.

"Because of my indiscretion, namely not following the fifth commandment, Peter gave me three choices. The first one of the choices consisted of being a rich California girl who had inherited her parent's money and traveled to Europe. I already mentioned the Rome incident to Father Joe." She looked at the other priests and they nodded in understanding. They looked serious now but perhaps they had lost interest and were mentally planning their Sunday liturgies. "The second choice was also a life of wealth, but the family lived in Paris. My mother would have been a couture fashion model and my father a clothing designer. But I didn't pick that life. Experience had already shown me that rich families don't know more than poor families."

She watched Father Joe nod his head but she stopped talking for a second, realizing she had gone on for a long time. A quick study of their faces made her weigh exactly how much of her story sounded believable and how much of it would be considered part of a teenager's hormonal imbalance. They could have been playing poker for all the emotion they portrayed–like none. At this point, nothing in their countenance belied any belief in her tale. She needed to breathe. It wasn't like facing a firing squad and yet, all of a sudden, her shoulders felt tense and she didn't feel at ease. Take a breath, she told herself, inhaling a large amount of air and crossing her feet at the ankles. "St. Peter gave me another opportunity to learn acceptance and to appreciate my loving family by giving me this wonderfully tempting choice. He had said maybe the second wealthy family in Paris might work out better for me, but it was entirely my choice. I had free will, he said."

"Yes, free will," Father Joe nodded, looking across the room at Father Andrew.

"The third and final choice was to be a **poor** little girl in Panama City." Christina put emphasis on the word **poor** and instead of showing her own courage and moral character she reminded Father Joe of what wealth could have done in his life. His poor, grieving Mother had pleaded with him to go to law school instead of seminary, but the pamphlet from the monastery had shown photos from around the world. Free travel had sounded so much better than being stuck in a suburb of Dublin to an impressionable seventeen year old.

And the sound of life in Paris made their imaginations wander. Quiet thus far, Father George piped up with, "What I wouldn't give to see Notre Dame," with a wistful, far off look on his rugged face. "That architecture alone…"

Father Joe smacked his lips as if dreaming of some sort of French cheese. "The food, the food, oh my goodness, I would have chosen Paris by far. What did you tell St. Peter, that… that you wanted to ... come right back home to your parents here in Normal?" Sad to think American girls didn't know about Paris and the sophisticated culture revolving around a steaming cup of café au lait, pastries and baguettes slathered with pate. Father Joe finally smiled now thinking of croissants, fresh with butter and delicious strawberry jam. The thought of having a choice to redo everything sounded tempting, making the priests feel a version of collective, unspoken guilt that put them all on the same bonded wavelength, almost like those who enjoyed sharing scandalous tidbits from a previous day's soap opera. Undeniably, they began enjoying Christina's incredulous tale.

Teenagers however, thought Father Joe, are rarely ready to make the best decisions; after-all wasn't he a teenager when he signed up for the seminary? His heart almost skipped a beat thinking back to his poor mother and his inability to send her anything to help her before she passed away.

Christina could see they were starting to daydream and she wanted to get them back on track. "Hello? No, I didn't pick Normal. Are you kidding? That's why everything happened." Stay calm, stay calm, she told herself, they had to listen. "I don't understand any of this myself. St. Peter said I had the three choices because of his three denials of the Father. You know the story. It's from the Bible."

"Yes dear, The Gospel of John."

"Saint Peter said three was a good number and I would someday reach the glory of my destiny. He said living in God's kingdom is a giant gift of eternal promises. All promises that are eventually fulfilled and I dared to ask him how he knew that every promise is granted. Can you imagine, I asked him that? He told me that he sees it happen every time. He said, 'God was not selling appliances or over-priced timeshares on tropical islands.' This was my future. All I had to do was choose but I had to make up my mind fast. He even made a joke and said I should choose now, before the Second Coming!"

The three priests busted out laughing, and Father Andrew looked like he was almost tearing up when he asked, "Wow, did you guys hear that? I always knew God had a sense of humor, but St. Peter too?"

Father Joe raised his right hand to silence the other two laughing priests. "And you chose what my dear?" Father Joe secretly hoped for more Parisian daydreams but the clock had loudly diverted her attention when it struck three. Christina was about to tell them how she had chosen poverty over Paris because the first attempt in Rome did not work out. Logically, she had thought money and riches had kept her from entering Heaven. The weirdest part of being a wealthy California girl traveling around Italy had to do with the fact that she didn't have much time to enjoy all her expensive and posh possessions while touring the Vatican anyway.

Her parents here in Normal didn't have a lot of money. She needed to know the truth, but something deep within her gut told her that breaking the fifth commandment was the real reason for almost everything that had happened.

"Father Joe. Father Andrew, Father George...there is one peculiar thing I can't understand," She turned to look the other two in the eye, returning her gaze to Father Joe. I think I was supposed to forget each one of these episodes and I'm not supposed to remember anything about these previous..." She paused, thinking of the right word..."experiences." In other words, I think I'm supposed to learn a lesson and then continue with my life rather than have any recollection of this."

"We're glad you remember. Highly unusual mind you, but any time we have a peek into the Heavenly process it assists us with our own faith and teaching," Father Joe leaned over his desk, "Before you tell us which life you picked, can you describe the Gates of Heaven?"

"The enormous Gate was a beautiful shade of turquoise. It had a rounded top and bleachers next to it filled with mostly older people. I think they were waiting their turn. There also seemed to be touches of gold and clear walls all around the entire area protecting it from elements such as wind and rain."

"So tell us now what did you pick?"

Christina curled her hair around her finger and said, "I told St. Peter, I wanted to go to Panama. He immediately said it was a good choice because of the mild winters." Father Joe looked astonished, jerking his arm while sitting straight up, accidentally knocking the huge pile of church bulletins down into a disheveled mess onto the floor.

Chapter Five

All three priests' eyes were popping out of their sockets as they asked in almost perfect unison, "How did you get to Panama?"

Christina smiled and said, "Oh, I remember that, it was very spiritual and kind of exciting. I wasn't afraid at all. I received a blessing from St. Peter, and he held a scepter above my halo that touched my hair. A sparkle of light flashed and I was gone. My eyes saw something glittery and there were some swooshes around me swirling and turning me around and around. I heard him say, 'good luck and hope to see you soon'."

"You went to Panama without a passport? You had a halo? Did you take a boat through the canal?" Father Joe was asking a staccato series of questions, taking feverish notes and trying to make eye contact with his friends. But his eyes were slits. His faced seemed to change and his lips sort of drooped on both sides of his mouth.

Christina quietly said, "I was born there. I was born Christina Isabella–and we lived in a tiny flat in Old Panama. I looked quite different and had shiny, dark brown hair. My mother was Hortensia Olivia Allende and she washed clothes for a living. She was the sweetest woman you would ever meet. My grandfather had a tourist business selling Panama hats on the street corner and sometimes he asked my mother to help. We were very poor, but somehow we managed to be happy. My mother worked hard and sometimes she would pick bananas, mangoes and guavas to supplement our simple meals. Most of the time we ate beans." Christina stopped because she could see the three of them were looking at her oddly.

Christina bit her lip. They stared at her like approaching deer on a Texan highway. "What? You guys don't believe any of this," she said with a disappointed look on her adorable face. "I have been all over the world, I really met St. Peter and I really experienced all of these things just like I'm telling you. It was just as real to me as sitting here talking to you!" her outburst sounded a bit louder than she had anticipated. If they would only blink, she thought, looking away from their stares.

Father Joe cleared his throat and said, "Christina, we never said we didn't believe you. We're taking this all in. You have to admit, it's a bit of a wild story, especially because I know where you were born. I know your parents. Christina, do you know that your parents moved here to get you the best medical coverage? You had a heart murmur before you were even born. *Children's Memorial* in Chicago has the best heart surgeons and your Mother's obstetrician had said you might need surgery if you survived the birth. Do you know any of this?"

"No," Christina whispered. "That's why they moved to Normal, Illinois?" The only thing she remembered was something about bills. Once, when she had wanted something at the mall, her mother yelled at her about medical bills and how she had put them into debt before she was born. It was ages ago but she knew her dad hated balancing his checkbook. Father George and Father Andrew looked like they wanted to speak. The horrible realization that she had caused her parents so much grief from the outset made her dizzy.

"They wanted a 'normal' baby. Take a good look in a mirror–their prayers were answered."

Christina looked at the ground before taking a deep breath. Her foot played with a wayward bulletin. The thought that she almost hadn't even made it sent the small hairs on the back of her neck straight up. She loved her mom and dad so much that hindsight made all of her past complaints look almost ridiculous. Her heart was racing and pulsating in her ears. Still, she had to continue. There was more, a lot more and these three disciples needed to listen to all of it.

Swallowing hard, the tone of her voice squeaked, "Wow that explains a lot, but my adventures in Panama really happened, and you know what? My life in Panama is not any more wild than the crazy sounding story my current father tells about hiding under a white sheet with his friend as they crossed under a barb wired fence in a huge snow storm while escaping communist border guards holding machine guns!" There, she thought. She had made a true, verifiable statement at the expense of her lungs. Completely depleted, she inhaled, taking a deep, deep breath, fidgeting and knowing that none of her other statements would sound factual and even though they couldn't be checked out, they were as real to her as the nose on her face. The late afternoon sun dipped into the room bathing it with light.

"She has a point, Joe." Father Andrew calmly interrupted.

"OK, OK, we want to hear all of what happened. I just became a bit side-tracked." Father Joe said.

"Keep the faith all of you, let's listen," Father George interjected, as Father Joe stood to pull the shades down, keeping the sun's brilliant rays from blinding Christina.

As he sat back down and pulled in his chair he asked, "Where was your Panamanian father in all of this Christina?"

"My mother wasn't married," she paused, glancing up at Father Joe's eyes before she raised her eyebrows and contorted her lips. "Mamacita had a quiet boyfriend who worked at the cemetery. He was religious and felt very ashamed for getting mother pregnant. For the first few years of my life, I only saw my father through an iron fence near the church where he was digging graves for a living. My mother would point at him and say, 'there is your Papa!' When I was eleven, I dashed into the cemetery, grabbed his hand and pulled him towards mother. I told him, 'if you are my Papa then you belong in our home with Mama and me'. I told him to come with us immediately. I yelled and almost tore his filthy shirt by yanking on it. He wiped his forehead and stared at mother who kept screaming at me from across the fence to stop. I didn't stop; I kept yelling 'Papa, come home!' I cried and cried out loud like someone possessed." Christina paused for a brief second; realizing tears were running down her face. "The smell of freshly turned earth and my Father's sweat still permeate my memory. It's a smell I'll never forget." The clock ticked loudly and Christina inhaled. She wiped her face with the back of her hand. "Sorry."

"Did he come home to you?" Father Joe asked.

Almost in a trance, she thought back to that day which now seemed ages ago. Her eyes looked beyond Father Joe, beyond the wall of his office and back into her memory. "He laid his shovel down and grabbed me while he cried, 'Bueno, un poco de la mina. Si, mi tesoro, si.' He was kissing the top of my head and holding me as we ran out through the gate to my waiting mother. Now they were both crying, but I was so happy that we finally had a family." She recalled the hugs and the joyful kisses and finally smiled.

Baffled, Father Joe inquired, "*You speak Spanish and Italian?*"

But Father George raised his arm and asked, "You were really happy?"

"Oh yes, I had a good life with nice people. Though poor, we always seemed to have enough to eat. One time, my father, whose name was Gonzalo, went to a restaurant with me. He was very tall for being of Guaymi and Kuna background. Buildings in Casco Antiguo have electrical wires wrapped on the outside that sometimes droop into doorways. Sometimes these wires caused my father to stoop before he entered someone's business or home. He certainly didn't want to be tangled in the conveniences of faxes, telephones and electrical currents. I sure hope they get wireless service over there soon. One time, a loose wire singed father's Panama hat when he went to buy my mother some coffee beans. A spark had put a black hole on the crown, making it look like a bullet had passed through his head. After that, he joked about how I had saved his life–like a guardian angel–because he had held my hand when it happened."

Chapter Six

Christina stopped for a moment and looked around the cold, institutional office. It was three o'clock and she had a lot more explaining to do. "Can I be excused for a moment? I'll be back in two minutes." She needed to use the ladies room and wanted to get a drink from a drinking fountain. When she stood up, everyone smiled and seemed glad for the break too.

"What do you guys make of all this?" Father Joe looked at the door closing behind Christina. He got up, went to his tray of Waterford glasses and poured a drink. "Drink, Andrew? George?"

"No thanks, Christina just mentioned her father buying coffee beans and I think that set off my coffee cravings. I need caffeine," Father Andrew mumbled, rubbing his eyes. "That was a nice lunch place we went to, but I ate too much as usual," he said rubbing his stomach.

Father George laughed and looked longingly at the drink, but asked, "Do you have soda or water?"

"Only whiskey here, but there's a soda-machine in the foyer." Father Joe's guests weren't helping him. "Well? Is this huge or just childish fantasy? What do you guys think? Do we keep this under wraps or bring it to the diocese?"

"Excuse me, while I get a cola. I'll be right back, Joe." Father Andrew stood. "Can I bring you one as well?" he asked Father George.

"Yeah, I'd like that. Thanks." He dug around in his pocket for change, but Father Andrew was almost out the door when he turned and said, "Don't worry about it, I got this one."

Tiny droplets of perspiration beaded around Father Joe's neck, under his white clerical collar. Maybe he was taking this all too seriously; after all, this girl could be hallucinating or taking drugs. He wanted to talk to George and Andrew in the short time she was out, but they seemed to be preoccupied with quenching their thirst. Every minute they didn't confer about this unusual situation could ignite chaos. Usually slow to anger, a fuse erupted inside making him sweat profusely.

At the cola machine, Father Andrew's canned soda clunked down into his waiting hands. He bought another one and saw Christina step around the corner. "Can I offer you a soda, Christina?"

"No, I'm fine; I just found the water fountain."

He smiled, and said, "Ask and you shall receive."

"Seriously, I'm good." she paused and slowed her steps, waiting to accompany him back to Father Joe's office.

"Have you always been this creative?" Father Andrew asked. He wore a leather jacket over his regular black shirt and khaki pants. To Christina he seemed like a fairly nice guy, but his question threw her for a loop.

"How do you mean creative? Everything I've said is true. I have no reason to make up stories. In fact, if you're the same Father Andrew from Chicago I think you are, then you are the famous novelist/priest who makes up stories for a living. Well? Am I right?" He nodded affirmatively, but waited for her to finish. She looked him straight in the eyes and said, "I'll swear on any Bible that this is not fiction, this is my life. If anyone is creative around here it's you!"

"Wow," he laughed. "Are we being a bit touchy and defensive Christina? Just like everything–even with faith, there has to be some basic element of comprehension. Typically, priests interpret scripture and biblical passages that have already been analyzed by every Pope and Vatican official for hundreds of years. New information needs to be handled in a precautionary and introspective way with reason—and all new material is usually interpreted based on a middle ground of understanding. Please don't let me influence any part of how you feel, regarding these things that happened to you. We are very glad to learn more, just remember it is new to us too. We only know what you're telling us. Your story is a new one and by the way, you are the only person I've ever met with such insight into the afterlife." He opened the door and followed her in.

Thankful to be around the others, she immediately noticed that Father Joe wasn't looking very well. In fact, he was as red as a stop sign. The analogy literally made her think maybe she should stop and continue another time. "Father Joe, are you okay?" she asked, taking her place in the leather chair.

"Yes, I'm fine, just a bit warm I guess." He brushed his bangs from his face and smoothed down hairs that straggled and clumped together, due to the moisture creeping up from his collar. "Everything is great; now let's continue along from where we left off," he declared impatiently.

"Father George agreed it was warm as well, and removed his light jacket.

"It's not warm here at all. Try spending a lifetime in Panama where the average temperature is over 80 degrees. This is actually cold." Christina looked around and saw vacant, disbelieving stares. Were they ever going to believe her? Sure, she was creative but she was nothing compared to God. God was the creative one and she had to show these three just how creative He was.

Father Andrew popped the can of soda and asked, "A lifetime?"

Chapter Seven

"The ocean breezes kept us cool." Christina closed her eyes so she could recall the vivid colors, the flowers and the sounds that had filled her recent memories. "My father in *Panama* loved to sit by the steps near the *Plaza de Francia. He'd* listen to the waves lap at the concrete walkway where children play and giggle and throw rocks into the water below. Vines grow over the walkway, creating an arbor, providing shade, so lovers and families can enjoy a stroll while taking in the view towards *New Panama*. It's very charming and even though the cruise ships sail by and allow hundreds of passengers to visit on a daily basis it's still wonderful…." She sighed wistfully.

Father Joe watched her eyes, her motions and he kept thinking she looked like she spoke from some deep trance, when he interrupted with, "Please explain. This Plaza, could you tell us more about it and describe it?" He held a pencil above his yellow pad ready to jot some notes.

"Of course. It's near the promenade–or *Las Bovedas* where the statue of a rooster sits atop a tall pedestal in the French Plaza. Tourists, who have visited, know the area well—it's very pretty. There are three lights on each streetlamp and small blooming white flowers skip along the rocks facing a fence with magnificent swirls, fleur-de-lis, curlicues and intricate ironwork. The flowers and the ironwork seem to hold everything together. It's a very pleasant and relaxing place.

"Sounds lovely, did you say there is a rooster?" Father Andrew asked quietly.

"Yes, Father," she opened her eyes and continued. "My Dad worked so hard burying the local poor and indigent. He used to tell me it seemed like rich people didn't die because he never buried any. It was a running joke— I know it's kind of morbid—but it made everyone smile. Mom would crack up every time he'd say something about a famous rich person on television that would live forever. Of course, the reason my dad never buried any rich people is that the cemetery he worked at was in the poorest section of town. When I was sixteen, I told him I wanted to be rich so I wouldn't have to die and maybe I could live forever," she smiled, but worried the priests would laugh. "Anyway, I almost did become rich. One day I was at my cousin's confirmation where I met a lady determined to introduce me to her cousin. Later....Oh, much, much later, she introduced me to Jaime Mancuso."

He wrote Jaime Mancuso on his pad of paper and looked up. "...And he was?" Father Joe inquired, noticing Christina's now blushing cheeks.

"He owned a bunch of businesses in *Curacao*. He grew up in *Panama City* and was around thirty-five years old and he thought he was the coolest guy in Central America. His aunt was that lady I had met at my confirmation."

"What kind of business, Christina?" Father Joe kept on taking copious notes. The redness was fading and though he appeared more relaxed, his fingers flew across his yellow pad.

"I'm still not entirely sure, but it had something to do with tourism. The day we met, I was standing near some Kuna Indians selling their images and molas to photographers off the big cruise ships. I had brought cookies to my dad's auntie. One day later, Jaime came to my parent's house on Saturday afternoon asking for my hand in marriage. Before he even said a word, my mother, Hortensia, burst into tears and left the room."

Father Andrew wanted to know something and asked, "Had you even heard of *Curacao* up to this point?"

"What difference does that make?" Father Joe snapped, but he kept scribbling with a furious passion, like a mad monk.

Father Andrew remained quiet, noting Father Joe's exasperated demeanor.

"Actually, I had heard it was an island ruled by a Dutch queen." Christina beamed in a childlike manner when discussing the memory, "In fact, Jaime proposed that evening and promised me a life similar to that of a carefree princess, full of luxurious surroundings, parties, tropical gardens and flamingos. I was to live in a giant mansion on an estate filled with yellow hibiscus flowers and birds of paradise, near Willemstad." She sighed, reliving the dream in her mind.

"Well, that sounds tempting…what happened? Your description of the mansion and flamingos would entice almost anyone. "Good looking chap?" *Maybe things were going to get interesting after all,* he thought.

Christina laughed. "No, that wasn't it."

"Didn't you accept his proposal?"

Still giggling, Christina tried calming down but she nervously swung her feet, crossing them at the ankle in scissor-like kicks. After all, these were inappropriate adult memories and now, here she was a child again. "I said I would go and become his bride because I had never been anywhere. In all my excitement, I didn't hesitate, even though mother never stopped crying. Jaime purchased the most amazing wedding gown with Austrian lace and silk ties at the waist. My Father, Gonzalo said I looked like an angel standing in *Iglesia San Jose.* That was our family church and it has a giant golden altar. The altar has quite a history because it was rescued from some pirate called Henry Morgan. Anyway, it seemed the entire area of *Casco Antiguo* showed up on the day of our wedding. Ecstatic about finally being free of poverty and the chains binding me to the poorest section of *Panama,* I felt ready to embark on my new life and a new journey. I felt like a bird sailing above the jungle, finding a better place to land. As the music of Mendelssohn played the Wedding march on the organ, all I could think about was how my family had worked so bitterly hard their entire lives and how they would never afford many of the luxuries I was already beginning to enjoy."

"You felt guilty?" Father Andrew managed to ask.

She nodded and listened to Father George who looked at her and said, "I'm sure you were beautiful and excited, but I see something missing in this part of your story."

"Stop it George, she's doing a good job of filling us in," Father Joe retorted, shuffling sheets of paper.

"But..." Father George had a question, and though important, it seemed like it was no use. Joe continually cut him off.

"Please, my child, continue." Father Joe prompted.

"Yeah, well I was going to leave on a short flight to *Curacao* the next morning from the *Marcos A. Gelabert International Airport.* Jaime had pointed it out on the map and he told me we would have a taxi zipping us up the *Avenida de los Martires* to *Diablo north....*"

"Another taxi? Don't tell me you die in a crash again?"

She waved her hand and shook her head. "No, no. This wasn't like that first time."

"Timeout. Can we finish the part about the wedding first?" Father Andrew interjected. Father Joe shifted a bit in his chair and wondered why Andrew would sidetrack her from rewarding two miserable days of total malarkey with potentially juicy tidbits that might describe a honeymoon.

"Yes, of course," Christina enjoyed talking about most of it but a serious pallor came over her face when asked to return to the wedding discussion. "My mother's sobbing filled every inch of that crowded sanctuary," she said sullenly. Tears, rimmed Christina's eyes but she felt determined not to cry again in front of three priests. Guys thought crying was weak and stupid. They would be convinced she was just being creative. Lord, help me, Christina mumbled to herself before proceeding.

Tired of being stepped on, Father George became bold. "In hindsight, Christina," he asked, "do you know why your mother cried so much?"

She raised both of her hands to her burning cheeks and blinked back the moisture about to drip from her lids. Maybe it was warm in the office. "Yes, Father George, because she knew…she knew I didn't love him."

Chapter Eight

"Ah, the maternal instinct, very interesting..." Father Andrew leaned back in his chair and crossed one leg over his thigh.

"So then...Christina...please go on." Father Joe was trying to keep everyone from going off on a tangent. If they didn't stick to the subject, this meeting could last into eternity and he had plans this very evening. Mrs. Morgan, one of his Eucharistic ministers had invited him to dinner and he needed extra time to pick up a bottle of '***two buck chuck***' from *Trader Joe's*. It was his favorite store, mostly because of the word Joe in the name. He used to call himself 'Trader Joe' whenever he worked the Pentecost carnival, or when he volunteered to help the ladies at the thrift shop. Tonight's dinner was supposed to be a backyard barbecue and he was looking forward to some St. Louis style ribs. If he didn't make it to the Morgans' he was afraid of being called 'Traitor Joe'."

"It was all too much for my Mother, Hortensia." Christina continued, with a lump in her throat. "After exiting the church as a married couple, we knew we would have to return for more photographs and painful goodbyes. All of a sudden, we heard a huge commotion and a group of about twenty-five people stood above someone near the front. We went back up front to see what was the matter and it was mother. Can you imagine her heart had stopped pumping?" Christina placed her hand over her heart. "Some doctor tried to resuscitate her, but it was too late. She had become overwrought with so much anxiety and emotion that it killed her. The priest, who married us, buried her outside the window on the right side of the church. It was so incredibly sad." Christina inhaled deeply, pausing slightly but appearing slightly older or maybe just sadder. "Even though everyone told me to proceed with my new life as planned, I knew I couldn't leave my dad alone… with no one to take care of him. Jaime came to visit often, but we never really spent any considerable time together. It was as if we were never married.

I guess I interpreted my mother's death as a strong sign from God. I felt I belonged in old Panama with the old buildings that kept getting new coats of colorful paint now and then. The pain inside me chipped away like that paint, revealing a lonely person who remained part of the everyday background in the vibrant bay-front colonial city."

Father George looked down at his shoes. He didn't know what to say, but thought long and hard about the things she had expressed. She sounded so mature and to him her story sounded realistic and more than sad. The words she used were eloquent and heartfelt. He couldn't imagine anyone making any of this up especially after watching her childlike face express such deep emotions. Father Andrew also looked very serious but wanted to hear more of her vivid journey to another life. Both priests could tell Father Joe wasn't buying any of it so they decided not to interrupt for a while but Christina saw Father George mouth the word 'wow' and she noticed Father Andrew biting his lip.

Father Joe rubbed his hand over his bald spot. "Was it consummated?"

Suddenly a blank look washed her face free of her nostalgic feelings. She had no idea what that meant. "Excuse me?"

"Joe, shut up," Father Andrew said with a scolding, exasperated tone.

Father Joe raised his right hand sweeping down as if shooing a fly. "This is important. Christina, did you and Jaime sleep in the same bed together as a married couple?"

She bit her lip and knew what he was getting at. "Nooo." Didn't they understand she was talking about a different life? She had become a different person and she shouldn't be responsible for the indiscretions of a previous life. She hunched her shoulders and thought back to some mild petting and French kissing in the plaza. Oh my God, this was becoming weirder by the minute.

"Relax dear," Father Andrew interjected. "Joe, you're making our young lady nervous. Let her tell it the way it happened."

"Jaime finally asked for a divorce and an annulment because he wanted to start a family. I think he was more interested in having an heir to the family business. It was so strange, that life. Remember, my dad originally didn't want to come home, my mother didn't want me to leave, and I married a man who only wanted heirs for his business empire? I wonder what would have happened had I left for Curacao with Jaime. I know I was a good daughter **and** I'm positive I respected my parents even though they were completely different from the ones I have here. Funniest thing is I loved my parents in Panama and having different parents never crossed my mind."

"Tell us what you did later in life." Father George took a chance at asking an innocent question.

"It seemed that the historic section of *Panama*, which is now a **World Heritage** site, became a popular tourist destination. As I grew older, I accepted my fate, which was to sell goods to the tourists on the street near the *French Plaza*. I sold Panama hats and prayed every day for my parents. I loved and missed them so much." Christina stared down at the floor littered with the large pile of church bulletins haphazardly spread under Father Joe's desk. She wondered why they hadn't been handed out at mass, and figured Father Joe must have forgotten to pass them out.

"Did you ever get married again, or have a boyfriend?" Father George asked.

"No never, Father George. I devoted my life to praying for my mother and helping others. With many cousins on my father's side, it seemed I always had someone to bake or cook for and they all needed assistance with everything. The children were growing and my rosary beads were getting worn out."

Something set him off. Perhaps her indirect mention of the Virgin Mary when she brought up the part about praying the rosary but something ignited Father Joe's anger, turning him into someone she didn't recognize. Christina enjoyed the attention of these smart and inspirational men, but nothing in her mind prepared her for Father Joe's diabolical metamorphosis.

"You sit here and tell all of us that this happened with that smug look on your face, as if you did not know how ridiculous all of this sounds. Can't you at least act like the grown-up young lady you are supposed to be?" He shuffled the notes on his desk and looked at them distastefully. The red color was filling out his cheeks again making him look like an angry chipmunk. "I don't understand how the Christina I knew became such a compulsive liar."

"Hey Joe," Father Andrew tried interrupting.

"No, this is blasphemous." Father Joe's voice took on a harsh tone and he slapped the palm of his right hand down on the wooden desk. "I cannot have her going around engaging other students with some of these off the wall notions she probably read in a book or saw on T.V. If you're trying to get into acting class and win an ***Academy*** *award*, Andrew and George might go along with this nonsense, but I don't want to have anything to do with your charade." Father Joe was becoming unreasonable and crankier by the minute. Christina thought he needed a strong drink to loosen some of the old-fashioned obstacles crawling around in his brain.

A surprised Father George said, "Yes, Christina, maybe we should finish this some other time."

"No way," Father Joe pounced verbally, like an ally cat, onto his friend George. "It is finished today." Christina noticed spittle on the desk in front of her and thought better of interrupting.

Father Andrew tried calming everyone by asking for patience and faith. "Look, why don't we let the young lady finish so she can at least get it off of her shoulders?" He smiled at Christina hoping she'd continue.

"I'm fine with that Joe," Father George looked at the priest sitting at the desk and began wondering why Joe always worked at the smaller parishes. Maybe he had been impatient with the Bishop. On the other hand, maybe he just liked it here in *Normal*. Then again, maybe he had some issues. Though he had known Joe for a long time, he had never seen his temper flare as it just had.

"Christina, tell us what else happened? We do want to know...." This time it was Father Andrew urging her to continue. Both Andrew and George were entranced by the mysterious account coming from the angelic faced young lady. If nothing else, the strange tale could perhaps be inspiration for his upcoming bestseller. He already had the advance from the publisher and his agent had listened to all of his latest ideas without sounding overly optimistic about the success of any one of them. He wondered if he could obtain his agent's legal counsel to obtain the rights to Christina's story. Considering that she was a minor, he needed to protect himself from some kind of infringement action or lawsuit. It was always better to be safe than sorry. He was almost defrocked over his steamy romance novel that had the misfortune to hit the *Times* bestseller list the same day a new Pope was elected by the *Vatican counsel*. No way was he going through any of that again. Monday, he would make some calls to his agent.

It was quiet in the office, and none of them wanted to break the silence. The only sound was Father Joe blowing his nose into a tissue and then fiddling with his notes. Father Andrew kept daydreaming to fill the void. Perhaps he'd call his next novel, '*Christina's Story*.' His agent would love this stuff.

"Are you guys sure? I don't want to make anyone mad," she almost whispered.

Father Joe stood up and stretched his legs. He pulled the shade a bit farther down, and sat again. Knowing he was being watched by two esteemed colleagues from Chicago, both of whom had the ear of the Bishop, gave him an uneasy feeling. He decided to adjust his attitude, so he could endure more of Christina's teenage fantasy. When he had pulled the shade down, he noticed a mourning dove pecking quietly on the window. Dismissing what normally he'd interpret as a sign of peace, he sat, moving his chair closer to the desk making a hullabaloo, kicking bulletins on the floor aside and displaying obvious signs of negative body language. Sounding a bit terse and as smooth as a pebble-filled driveway, he finally spat out, "All right, all right, go on. What happened next?"

She could tell Father Joe was forcing himself to listen. "Not much more in *Panama*, except I lived to be eighty-five years old. I always thanked God for everything and I'm hoping he forgives me for whatever I did wrong. It was a long life and I learned about the important things that really mattered." She wasn't sure if she should continue, so she crossed her arms and put her hands in her lap, waiting to be prompted, like an obedient child.

"That's it?" Father Joe asked as patiently as possible.

Christina looked at the clock above Father Joe. "No, there's a bit more."

Chapter Nine

Father Andrew looked at her with an intensity that made her feel almost uncomfortable. "What do you mean you saw the things that mattered?" He wanted to make eye contact with her so he could stare into her soul. He tilted his head searching her face and though he kept staring, she looked away.

"I saw that family, truth, honesty and patience are part of His plan and not ours, regardless of free will. We can choose, but His plan takes control of our fate anyway." She finally looked at Father Andrew and a tender smile came over her delicate features.

"Pretty good, for a sixteen year old, isn't it? Father Joe was starting to show his sarcasm again.

"Joe, please give her a chance to finish." Father Andrew felt *he* had to take control if they wanted to get to the bottom of this story and take something concrete away from this day. He placed his cola can on the floor under his chair. "Christina," he asked, "how did you manage to get here? Back to Normal?"

"When I finally died of old age in *Panama*, I awoke from my sleep in front of St. Peter again."

"Really?" Father Andrew was leaning forward in his chair.

"Yes, really," Christina felt this was the best part of the whole explanation. "St. Peter looked very wise with small, up-turned corners on his lips that made his masculine face light up with happiness and love. I told him he must find it amusing that I had just wasted eighty-five years in a third-world country, trying to figure out my mistakes. He said that I had done very well; he also said that God's time is like a liquid that can freeze or flow accelerating years into our earthly seconds. Like Genesis for example, He made the world in seven days but His days are different.

Although it wasn't really a test, I guess I hadn't wasted any time. He was very proud of the fact that even though I was poor and lonely, I also figured out that love was the most important lesson of all. He reminded me that I had died in the middle of saying the Lord's Prayer. Then I asked him why I wasn't in Heaven already and he said that in my case I could either apply all of the things I learned to my life here and complete the incomplete, or I could go in front of God and enter the kingdom of Heaven immediately."

Excited, Christina moved her feet and smiled. "I was shocked to find out that I could choose to go to Heaven, or resume and pick up my life where I had left off and all I had to do was ask. He scratched his gray beard and asked me if I had been happier rich or poor? I told him—honestly– that I thought being content with the life you are given seems to be the closest anyone gets to happiness. He asked me if I remembered the story of the rooster and how he, St. Peter, had denied Jesus before the cock crowed three times. Of course, I was familiar with the famous passage from Matthew in the Bible; that section reminds everyone how hard it is to be human. Then he asked if I remembered the rooster on the fresco in the *Vatican*? I nodded. Then he asked if I remembered the rooster above the *French Plaza* in *Panama*? Again, I nodded. He told me very seriously that as soon as I see a third and final rooster I will forget this whole story and I will be forgiven." She held up three fingers while speaking. "After St. Peter finished saying this last bit about the rooster, a huge wind picked me up and brought me into Father Joe's confessional. I had to float through some ice cold clouds and that's how I got here." She shivered at the memory.

"Have you seen the rooster, a third rooster?" Father George asked.

"No, I haven't," Christina, continued, "But listen—I answered Father Andrew's question, that's how I got here. I didn't even get a chance to say goodbye to St. Peter. The wind carried me through the sky, ripped away my angel wings, silky gown and halo, then dressed me in my regular school clothes, bringing me here to all of you. I hope you accept my confession," she said, averting her eyes and looking down at the floor full of bulletins. "How many Hail Mary's do I have to say Father Joe?" She leaned down, picking up a small stack of those that edged out from under the desk. The only sound in the room was the ticking of the clock, but she could hear Father Joe wheezing a bit due to his heavier breathing. Then, quietly she placed a neat pile of the bulletins in front of her on the desk and looked at him for a response.

"Oh, for goodness sake, I don't know, we have to think about it. Why don't you come back tomorrow Christina?" Father Joe looked at his friends and they all seemed to agree that they would come back the next day. It was six o'clock and time for everyone to catch a train, and for Christina to head home for dinner. They stood and Father George put his windbreaker on. Even though her small house on Shepherd road was only a short walk up the street, her growling stomach made her wish for wings.

"Bye, Father Andrew, see you tomorrow Father George." She shook their hands, and waved goodbye to Father Joe. After driving the two others to the station, he stood alone in front of his parish on Fort Jesse Road. Father Joe stared at a long shadow casting a profile of what looked like Jesus with his out stretched arms on the side of the church. Inside his chest, he felt a loud almost perceptible throbbing. The image on the wall actually frightened him, "Nonsense," he told himself. He had to get to the Morgans' barbecue. They made the best sauce and he loved her bacon infused cornbread. Later that evening, Father Joe got down on his knees to say his prayers and wondered about the implications regarding Christina's imaginary tale. What would happen, he pondered, if all, or most of it was true.

Chapter Ten

The next afternoon, Father George and Father Andrew had rushed back to Normal on the early afternoon train. They were excited about all the information the young girl had shared with them. Their conversation on the short journey included comparisons to visions children had in Fatima and Lourdes. Father Andrew had brought a tape-recorder, and was planning to bring Christina to Chicago to meet the Bishop. Her testimony of religious sightings could offer hope to hundreds of suffering individuals losing their faith. This was the injection their church needed. Not wanting to have an agenda but incapable of being someone different from who he was, he also thought this could be the foundation for a best seller, one he needed badly. They almost flew into Father Joe's awaiting car at the station.

"Hey, how was the trip?" Father Joe started the car. It was a beige Volvo with 259,000 miles on the odometer.

"Fine, except we were a bit rushed due to traffic." Trying to keep their anxious excitement to a minimum, they continued with small talk about the weather and the train amenities. "How about you? Anything new since last night?"

He chocked the vision of Jesus on the side of the church to shadows playing with his mind—but later that evening he had a powerful dream. "Not really, but I'm feeling strange about this whole thing. Our little parish can't handle the publicity. Imagine what would happen if this leaked out?" He turned on the blinkers and turned into the church parking lot. "Don't you remember what happened in Medugorje? Thousands flocked to the tiny village...."

"Yeah, we remember, Joe" Father George interrupted. "I've been there."

Father Andrew laughed, "Heck people even pay big money on EBAY for granola clusters shaped like Moses holding stone tablets."

"I guess I'm just worried about my generous parishioners. I don't want anyone taking advantage of their kindness," Father Joe said as he led the way into his office. "Besides, I had a horrible dream last night."

"You saw St. Peter?" Andrew quipped.

Father George laughed. "No," Father Joe explained. "It was us in purgatory. Sadly, I think Christina was there too."

"Oooh, tell us more," they smiled and followed each other inside.

"I will, but hold on for a second. There's a lot going on."

"Well, to be perfectly honest with you Joe, I'm kind of excited." Father Andrew said, searching the room for a plug for his tape-recorder. "Don't worry, this won't be another Fatima for goodness sake, have some faith. This is probably the most exciting thing to happen in Normal, Illinois. It could be the economic boost this area needs right now."

The office lights were off. Father Joe went to the window first, opening the blinds. It was ten minutes after four. Then he stood up, walked back towards the door and turned on the overhead lights before sitting down at his desk.

"Now, tell us about your dream, Joe." Father Andrew always loved tales of intrigue.

"Wasn't she supposed to be here at four?" Father George asked, as he took his place on the foldout chair.

"Don't worry, any teenager wanting as much attention as she does will be here." He shuffled more bulletins and decided to tell them about his dream while waiting. "Drink anyone?" Father Joe needed one, but waited for them to gently decline. He enjoyed their company, but thought they were a wee bit pedantic. The scholars he knew weren't as serious as these two and all his friends in school drank wine and scotch like giant beluga whales being released from captivity. They were bigger actors than Christina–all a bunch of phonies. Didn't they see this hoax for what it really was? He took it to be a young girl's desperate cry for attention. Why did they need to drag this out for almost a week now? Didn't they have better things to do than hang out in his parish?

"All right, let me tell you about my vivid dream," he began. *Covered with something like mulch or brown trash that had gone through some sort of recycling machine or wood chipper, the soil we were walking on felt spongy under our feet. Twilight hid the sun, and four of us were carrying something light but awkward on a path to a nearby location. No one grumbled or complained; they looked at their feet and marched like zombies down the dark path. 'Wait,' I yelled, picking up a nice leather wallet. 'Look, it's cash.' I quickly took the money, pocketed it and tried keeping up, when I saw another wallet and it too appeared to be bulging and full of dollars. 'Here,' I said to the guy next to me who I supposed was one of you two. 'Take it.' I handed him the money and noticed there were wallets all around the edges of the trail. We made it to our destination where the rest of the group immediately began to assemble whatever it was we had carried down the lane. While I scoped the area for more wallets, I overheard one of them make a crack about the stupid tart.*

'You mean me, don't you?' Christina said, stepping into view. Fine, I'm out of here.' she had said. Indignation boiled

in my veins. She appeared to check out the others and made negative judgements about our lifestyles. No one looked like upstanding individuals. She didn't want to hang out with us any longer than she needed to. Plus, she didn't like our language or being called stupid– and while I may have thought it yesterday–you all know I didn't say it.

In this nightmare, we certainly weren't men of the cloth. We were regular men, possibly evil men and Christina was worried she had entered into a gang of bad men. I decided to run, but the farther I traversed from the group, unusual signs made it clear, I shouldn't have left. I kept coming across more wallets, overstuffed purses and dusty luggage along the side of the road. Some were empty and filled with old clothes and fancy shoes. Frustrated and still angry– I finally realized this was purgatory, maybe even hell–and the money wasn't going to buy any of us a thing."

"That's quite a dream. Did you eat something spicy last night?"

Father Joe smiled. "Yes, as a matter of fact, I had the best ribs this side of Heaven."

"Did you ever figure out what you were carrying?"

"Nah," Father Joe shook his head trying to blink it all away.

"Well then don't worry about it. That kind of thing can happen to anyone. You're a good man Father Joe and these are tough times. Father George kept looking at the clock while still being compassionate. "Don't let it creep you out–best to forget about it."

Father Andrew cleared his throat and decided to tell his friend what he really thought. "Joe," he risked the pastor's anger, but had to speak his mind. "Joe, I think all of this really happened. I'm not talking about your strange dream. I mean Christina. I believe her. In fact, I had an epiphany if you will, last night too."
The others turned toward Andrew who was actually unplugging

his tape-recorder. "I don't even know why I brought this stupid thing considering my thoughts about this whole incident."

Father Joe glanced up and shrugged, "See, you probably feel like I do. You know it's a bunch of mumbo-jumbo too." He stared at the mess accumulating on his desk and played with a blue pen. "It's just like my nightmare. Pure fiction."

"No, that's not what I said, Joe, I said, I believe her. I think she didn't honor her parents and she broke the fifth commandment." Father Andrew was winding the cord around the bundle and placing it into a large brown carryall tote bag that also had a bottle of water. He pulled out the bottle and took a drink. "Think about it you guys; she told us all these details and described St. Peter, Panama and the Vatican with information she didn't exactly read on Wikipedia or FACEBOOK. The part about the rooster really intrigues me; in fact, it could be the literal key we've been searching for."

Father Andrew didn't raise his voice, but a passion filled him, making him glad he was a priest. "Joe, everyone breaks commandments all the time, but they don't end up meeting St. Peter and I doubt many of them get a second chance at eternal life."

"Wait," Father George wanted to understand, so he cut in. "You mean you honestly believe her? I thought I was the only one who thought her story sounded credible. I think she was telling the truth too."

"We'll let the Bishop decide," Father Joe stated, while nervously shuffling papers and the small pile of old bulletins Christina had put on his desk. He made a small stack, placing them into one corner and slowly began putting other papers into drawers.

"She's not coming Joe, I'm telling you. I think she learned her lesson the hard way, but she definitely learned it." Father Andrew put the bottle of water back into the bag and balanced the bag against the desk. "Acknowledging our errors is the first step in learning anything before we plod ahead into the unknown, thinking we know everything. What good is learning that we made a mistake, if we can't admit we were wrong? We're all sinners, right? The trick is to learn from our past. If there's one thing you might gain from that horrific nightmare you had last night, it's to open your eyes to the darkness ahead. Don't you think I'm right about this? Joe, I've known you for years and I can't believe how stubborn you are!"

The clock ticked loudly above Father Joe who kept working intently on filing his old bulletins, avoiding the gaze of the other men while emptying trays and placing documents into drawers and the trash can under his desk. Father Andrew seemed annoyed with Father Joe looking at his papers instead of listening to his comments. "Can't you see how great this is? I've listened to many confessions throughout my years and thousands of people wish they could have a do-over." His mind reeled with the possibilities and whether Christina pushed a wrathful God or tested the limits of forgiveness.

"She's just luckier or maybe more innocent—God has a reason for this and maybe it's simply this: so we—-us three," he swept a finger around the room like a lasso–know the truth." The clock ticked loudly but Father Joe continued to shuffle papers, seemingly ignoring Andrew's assertive plea. Father Joe wanted to curse at both of them–couple of lying hypocrites—who only pulled out the best Irish whiskey or French cognac while in the company of fancy collared cardinals. By telling them his nightmare, he had bared deep psychological secrets by indirectly laying his soul on the line. Andrew probably even recorded all of it. For years, he had thought they were his friends. He felt withered, old and very alone.

At four-thirty, Father George stood up and stretched his legs. "Maybe we should call her. Do you have her number?"

"No," Father Joe didn't have her number, but he said, "Let's get this over with and go to her house. I know where they live." He grabbed his keys, stood, turned off the lights and headed back through the courtyard to the parking lot. Huffing and puffing, he looked like a man on a mission. Focused on finishing this investigation, he marched quickly, dashing through the door towards his old Volvo, not waiting for the other two priests who lagged behind and hurried to catch up. Father Andrew grasped the handles of his tote bag and followed Father Joe and Father George. He took large steps through the courtyard, and when he looked down, he noticed masses of downy white fluffy feathers strewn all over the grass.

Chapter Eleven

Unkempt grass and hedges that desperately needed trimming filled the front yard behind a small entry gate of the tiny home. Father Joe led the procession up a fractured walkway to the landing and knocked gently on the whitewashed door. Christina's mother answered, wearing a suit with an apron wrapped around her middle. Though she only opened it a small crack, incredibly delicious smells of home cooking wafted out the door, almost knocking the three holy men to the ground. That's when they collectively realized that it was probably a bad time to visit.

"Hello?" she spoke through a screen and looked at all three priests. Hesitating for a brief moment she said, "We sent our remittance last week, I think. Was this for the school paving or the general collection? Oh dear, I better ask Jan." She was a lovely, tired woman who looked stereotypically like a multi-tasking genius. Soft wisps of hair fell over her forehead, giving her the air of a woman who had triple booked all her appointments so she could fulfill some kind of personal ideal of superwoman. She looked determined and very capable. Mysterious eyes conveyed trust, faith and love. A youthful spirit sparkled from deep within. But her lovely eyes weren't easy to see because they were hiding behind smart but old-fashioned cat-eyed spectacles.

Father Andrew stepped to the front and said, "We're actually here to talk to Christina. Is she here?"

Dropping her protective guard, dimples appeared along with a smile. "Oh, I see. She's been such a surprising little angel today. Did she do something wrong? Normally, she doesn't like helping out in the kitchen. Please come in." Christina's mother held the door open for the visiting priests. She recognized the shorter Irishman from church, but wondered about the other two and worry began clouding over that twinkle in her eyes. "Christina," she yelled into the kitchen, "you have visitors."

When Christina came through the door of the kitchen, she looked different. Her hair was combed and she seemed to be dressed nicer than the previous two days. In fact, she wasn't wearing anything black. If they didn't know better, they would have thought it was a different person all together, a kind of long lost twin returning from overseas or something. Her gleaming eyes looked fresh and her cheeks were rosy. She looked happier and surprised, but slightly shocked to see them.

"Yes, mom, what did you say?" she had been busy setting the table for dinner. Her mind whirled with the notion that the three men would tell her mother and father things she didn't want them to know. It had been a confession. They had to respect her privacy. Worried they would divulge her intimate secrets, she made sure to keep the three of them in her line of sight at all times.

The divine aromas would have excited even the most jaded Chicago food critics. Father Joe wanted to invite himself to dinner and almost started to say something when Christina's mother saved the day by asking, "Would you gentlemen care to try some good ethnic food? It's a very simple peasant style dish, but my mother, Christina's grandmother, used to make it and we have fun trying to copy her old recipes. Besides, my husband is attending an award ceremony tonight, so we would enjoy the company. I always cook for more than three and tonight it would have only been two of us. We have plenty of food." Her suit had flour on the lapel, and she looked warm from standing over her stove. Her genuine kindness was apparent when she pointed towards the kitchen and said, "Christina, go get a bottle of wine for our visitors."

"Sure, Mom," Christina turned and went back into the small kitchen but stared through a small gap while managing to grab a few extra plates. She set three more settings and wanted to find the best wine they had in the house. It was nice to have company, and it seemed like they never entertained because her parents were always busy. She meant to ask her Mom about those crazy medical problems that brought them to the Chicago area when she got a chance. It was amazing to think that her parents moved to this town and this tiny house in order for her to live a healthy life. She could have died somewhere for lack of the best medical care. Simple words could not construct the gratitude she felt in her overflowing heart. While the what-ifs filled her mind with the obvious and potentially horrific outcomes, she grabbed napkins, forks and spoons along the way to the wine rack.

She heard her mother speaking, "Father Joe, I remember you from the church, but please introduce me to your friends." Irena removed her glasses and wiped her brow with the back of her arm. "You are staying aren't you?"

Father Joe inhaled the aroma and smiled. "We would be delighted to share your meal. Thank you for the generous invite." He couldn't believe his luck. Yesterday, the Morgans' barbecue and now, an authentic Polish feast. Life was good. "This is Father Andrew and Father George from Chicago. They are here to learn more about your daughter's harrowing escapades from the last few days."

Everyone shook hands with Irena and though they all looked like friendly faces, tension gripped her narrow, padded shoulders. She stared at Father Joe's pink-rimmed green eyes and tried to understand. "Harrowing? How do you mean?" Christina has been going to school and attending all her classes, as far as I know anyway," she said, blinking rapidly. She pursed her lips before calling after Christina to hurry with the wine. She observed her guests, sizing up Andrew's leather jacket and salt and pepper hair also noting that Father George seemed to be bashful and somewhat embarrassed. Then, she turned towards Father Joe. "Is there something I need to know?"

When Christina came through the door she said, "Mom, is this wine OK? This is the one the realtor gave you."

"Oh yes, this is as great an opportunity as any, let's open it now. Perfect." Christina's mother loved having an excuse to sip on a good glass of wine and felt honored sharing a bottle with three priests. She smiled a bit broader smile than usual and indicated where they should sit. "Please sit down Father Joe. You can sit over here." She pointed to the couch and went over to turn on the radio before she excused herself to return to the kitchen. The classical station played Beethoven's Sixth symphony and then changed to Puccini's famous aria.

"Christina," she whispered in her ear. "Please, go over there and sit down. Be a good hostess and keep them company. Is there something I need to know? They want to know about your 'harrowing' adventures. I think that's what they said anyway. What is that all about?"

Whatever the reason these men were here, she knew her daughter to be a smart, industrious student and a good girl when it came to boys. Nevertheless, her mother's intuition made her worry and she secretly wished her husband was home. Maybe it was time Christina realized that actions have consequences and becoming responsible is a step into adulthood. She swallowed a small regal giggle, turned and disappeared into the kitchen to tend to the amazing aroma that slipped under the door like a genie floating out of a bottle of fine Italian wine.

Chapter Twelve

"Harrowing? I'm not sure I know what that means." Christina worked diligently on the uncorking of the deep red wine. Her eyes went to the kitchen and her ears listened for sounds like the sink and the oven door. Her mother didn't need to hear this stuff. Though set on a low volume, the old Magnavox speakers shook with dramatic Italian lyrics. "O Dio vorrei morir, Babbo, pieta, pieta!" which only Father Andrew—a big fan of opera and especially Madame Butterfly, understood it to mean: "Oh God, I'd like to die! Father I beg of you, I want to die. Have pity on me Father!"

Father George stepped in, "Harrowing means something that disturbs you deeply."

Christina poured the wine four ways, and then ran to get herself a cola. The fourth glass was for her mother. She looked at the three priests and opened her eyes as wide as possible trying to make eye contact with all of them at the same time. In a soft voice she whispered, "Look, I can't talk about this in front of mom, so try to be understanding. I love my parents, and I don't want them to think about anything that would frighten them. Please?" Loudly she said, "Harrowing? Let's see...I guess moving is harrowing."

"You're moving Christina?" Father George asked.

"Yup, it's all set, we're moving 'cause my dad got a promotion at a different university. We already have a house, and I'm already enrolled in the new school. It's kind of exciting, but I suppose it could be called 'harrowing'."

Christina's Mother poked her head out of the kitchen. "Please everyone, have a seat at the dining room table. Dinner is almost ready."

Christina could hear Father Joe's growling stomach as he stood up and followed her to the antique dining table that she had set with utensils and placemats for five. He turned to Christina and whispered, "So, you're afraid of telling the truth in front of your mother? Maybe this would be a good time to put all your cards on the table young lady." He took his place at the head of the table, and stared at Christina as she put empty plates in front of each priest. "It's time to come clean and tell us all what you're really hiding."

A wolf dressed like a sheep, she thought. And the nerve– to talk like that in her home– prior to dining with her mother. Fortunately, the mysteries of time had taught her how to handle this and much much worse. Now all she had to do was respond while maintaining a cool attitude. "I'm not sure what you mean, Father Joe, I don't think I have anything to hide from my mom. What are you talking about?"

"Your story…tall tale…spiritual journey into la-la-land– you know exactly what I mean." Father Joe looked perturbed.

"Really, Father Joe, I have no idea what you mean." Christina put a plate in front of Father Joe, and turned to speak to some of the others who seemed to be anxiously waiting for the mouthwatering dinner. Her mother had made stuffed peppers and buttery biscuits but first she wanted to serve them an unusual chilled appetizer that required special, smaller plates.

Father Andrew, seemingly always an advocate, leaned in with a knowing smile as he took his place at the other end of the oval table. "He means, where are you moving?"

"Oh, that!" Christina exhaled and looked Father Andrew in the eye. "Sorry. My parents got new teaching positions in Arkansas with the University of Arkansas." Her mother came through the door and planted a kiss on Christina's cheek.

"My angel," she said while setting a giant bowl of her gastronomic talents on the center of the old table. "I'm so proud of her." Her eyes were glistening, satisfied with the carefully placed table settings, the folded cloth napkins and the steam rising from her own cooking. She was also thankful her daughter could hold the attention of these learned men in a grown-up discussion, while she wandered back and forth between the kitchen and the living room. As she sat down to join the group in saying grace, she said a small prayer to her own parents in Heaven and thanked them for teaching her the basics of modern motherhood. Her daughter was on track to follow in her mother's footsteps and for this, she was very, very grateful.

Meanwhile, way, way up above, sitting near the aqua-blue pearly gates of Heaven, St. Peter glanced down at the small group gathered around the dining table, far below in Illinois. He mumbled a prayer, and thought long and hard about letting any of the information Christina had shared with the church remain in their memories. Finally, he decided against it, and even though the general memories would be wiped clean, a divine trace of the lessons she had learned would always remain in her heart. There are nine other commandments, thought St. Peter and he knew he didn't have to worry about her for a long time—in Earth time—because primarily she's an incredibly sweet child and secondly, because she has a long Earthly life waiting around the corner. He knew one thing for certain; Christina would always honor her parents and never break the Fifth commandment again.

Christina looked around and felt something warm radiating up from her toes to her ears. Even though she wasn't drinking the wine, she saw a display of color reflect through the crystal glasses bouncing around the room just like the sun coming through the stained windows at church, a few days ago. Her mother once told her that when your ears are burning it meant someone was talking about you behind your back. Maybe Molly wondered why she hadn't called. It seemed like decades had passed since she saw everyone at school. She missed her teachers even though she had seen them yesterday. She missed her dad and her heart ached for old memories from Panama. Where were those people who had loved her? "Mom," she said. "I love you."

"I know dear," her mother answered, returning a hug. "I love you too."

"Where in Arkansas? I have family in Little Rock." Father George asked.

Father Andrew looked down at his appetizer plate. He picked it up, turned it around and grinned. "Irena, are these new?" Everyone looked down at the lively design of a bold and colorful rooster splashed across the center of each plate. The third rooster....

"Yes, Father, we'll need a few new things for our home in Hope, Arkansas. I chose the cute rooster design, because it reminds me of how early my husband gets up every morning."

"A toast," said Father George, holding up his glass. "A toast, to being human and new beginnings..."

# # #

Lightning Source UK Ltd.
Milton Keynes UK
UKHW011232091120
373077UK00006B/1105

9 781715 747312